MOJANG

MINECRAFT DUNGEONS

OFFICIAL STICKER BOOK

Written by Craig Jelley
Designed by Design Button
Cover Design by Andrea Philpots
Illustrations by Ryan Marsh

Special thanks to Alex Wiltshire, Kelsey Howard,
Sherin Kwan and Åsa Skogström

RANDOM HOUSE 🏠 NEW YORK

© 2021 Mojang Synergies AB. All Rights Reserved. Minecraft and the Minecraft logo are trademarks of the
Microsoft group of companies.
Published in the United States by Random House Children's Books, a division of Penguin Random House
LLC, 1745 Broadway, New York, NY 10019, and in Canada by Penguin Random House Limited, Toronto.
Random House and the colophon are registered trademarks of Penguin Random House LLC.
First published in Great Britain 2021 by Egmont Books, an imprint of Harper Collins Publishers
rhcbooks.com   minecraft.net
ISBN 978-0-593-37302-6
MANUFACTURED IN CHINA
13 12 11 10 9

RAVAGED LAND

Brave hero, the Arch-Illager's evil forces have brought darkness to this realm. We need you to help end his reign of terror. Identify the six differences between these Squid Coast scenes so we can begin to right his wrongs.

Answers are on page 32

LOOT DROP

Vanquishing these Illagers has left a ton of loot littering the ground, and— what sorcery is this? —it seems to be dropping in unusual sequences! Work out which item will drop next in each row and find the stickers on your sticker sheets to complete each one.

FEARSOME FOES

As you fill your inventory with heaps of loot, you notice a legion of mobs on the horizon blocking your path to the Arch-Illager. Read on to find out which mobs stand in the way of your quest. Then find the stickers to complete each of the cards.

CREEPER

A ticking green time bomb with a short fuse. Get too close and it'll explode in your face and take half your health points with it.

SPIDER

The creepiest of crawlies, the spider lurks in dark corners and traps you in its webs so it can lunge with its fangs to really cause damage.

SKELETON

The bony banes of many heroes, skeletons are a common sight, and have a habit of sniping you with a bow and arrow from distance.

ZOMBIE

The undead have risen, and they're on the hunt for fresh heroes. This common mob often comes clad in armor, making it a tricky foe.

CHICKEN JOCKEY

Chickens have been commandeered by baby zombies across the land, making the undead beings even more annoying.

BABY ZOMBIE

Like a zombie but still in training. They're a lot quicker than their fully grown counterparts, which makes them even more of a threat!

CHICKEN JOCKEY TOWER

Now, this is just getting silly. If you attack the chicken, the cute but deadly baby zombies might tumble to the ground and scatter before they cause too much trouble . . . maybe.

NECROMANCER

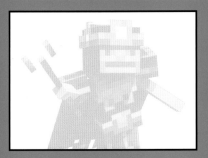

So THIS is where all the zombies and skeletons have come from! Necromancers have the power to raise the dead and cause carnage. But why are they working with the Arch-Illager?

HUSK

A zombie by any other name would be just as evil. The husk prefers warmer climates but is as much of a pain as its zombie cousin!

WITCH

This mob concocts potions in a cauldron and only stops to chase down would-be heroes. It pelts players with the deadly brews or drinks them to heal itself.

ENDERMAN

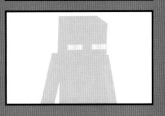

A slender terror with the power of teleportation. The enderman 'ports away from threats and can cause heavy damage to players.

SKELETON HORSEMAN

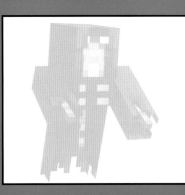

The fastest mob on four legs: this skeleton rides a matching bony steed into battle. They attack in packs of four, loosing arrows wildly.

WRAITH

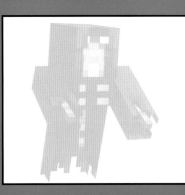

These floating specters can conjure searing blue flames around heroes and teleport away from them if in danger.

SLIME

A heaving, gelatinous terror that can split into smaller versions of itself. The only mob that can become a horde on its own!

CAVE SPIDER

Dwelling in the dankest caves, this spider is notable for its bluey-black hue. Still has an annoying web attack, though . . .

LOCATION SCRAMBLES

You stumble upon a notebook full of information about different locations. Unfortunately, all the names are written in gibberish. Decode the anagrams and place the correct sticker for each location to find out all about them.

QUITS AS COD

_____ _____

WORSE PROCEED

_____ _____

PUMAPUP STINKERS

_____ _____

WASPS GO GYM

_____ _____

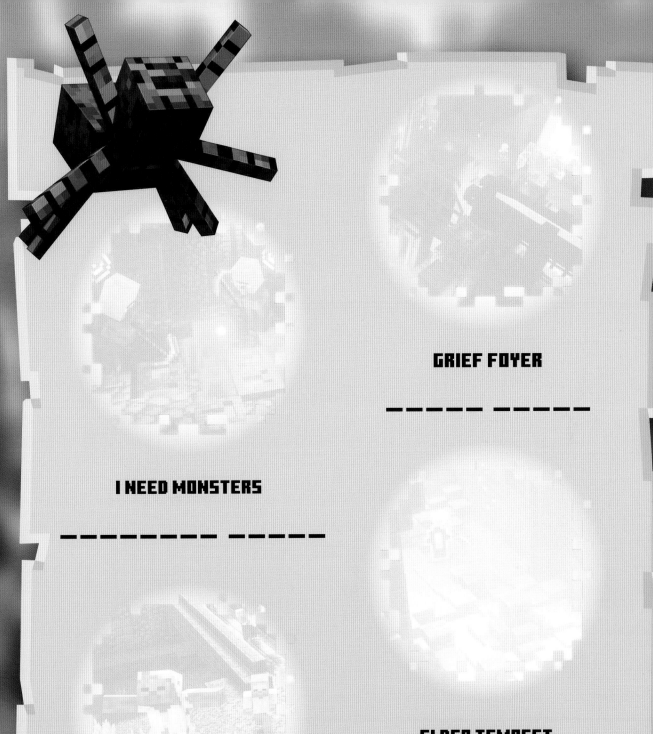

GRIEF FOYER

_ _ _ _ _ _   _ _ _ _ _ _

I NEED MONSTERS

_ _ _ _ _ _ _ _ _   _ _ _ _ _ _

ELDER TEMPEST

_ _ _ _ _ _ _ _ _   _ _ _ _ _ _

OAT CAN CYNIC

_ _ _ _ _ _   _ _ _ _ _ _ _

INVENTORY MANAGEMENT

You've been cleaving your way through hordes of mobs and collecting more loot than you can handle. Use the shaped loot stickers from your sticker sheet to fill the spaces in your inventory.

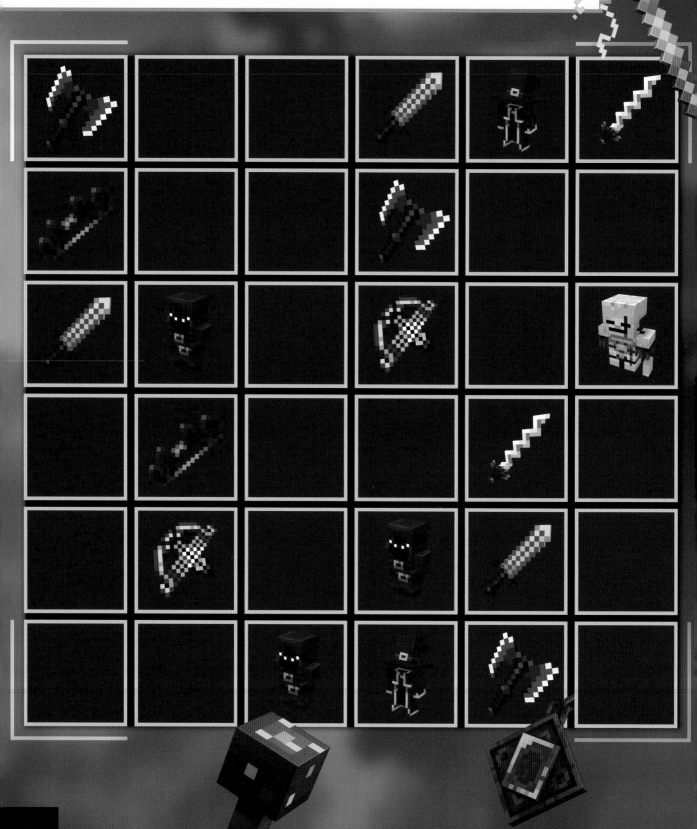

SOUL-DOKU

Your quest has been getting increasingly more difficult as you get closer to the Arch-Illager, but fortunately, you've just discovered some Artifacts—soul-fueled items with untold powers. See if you can fit the Artifact stickers in this grid so there's only one of each type in every row, column, and block.

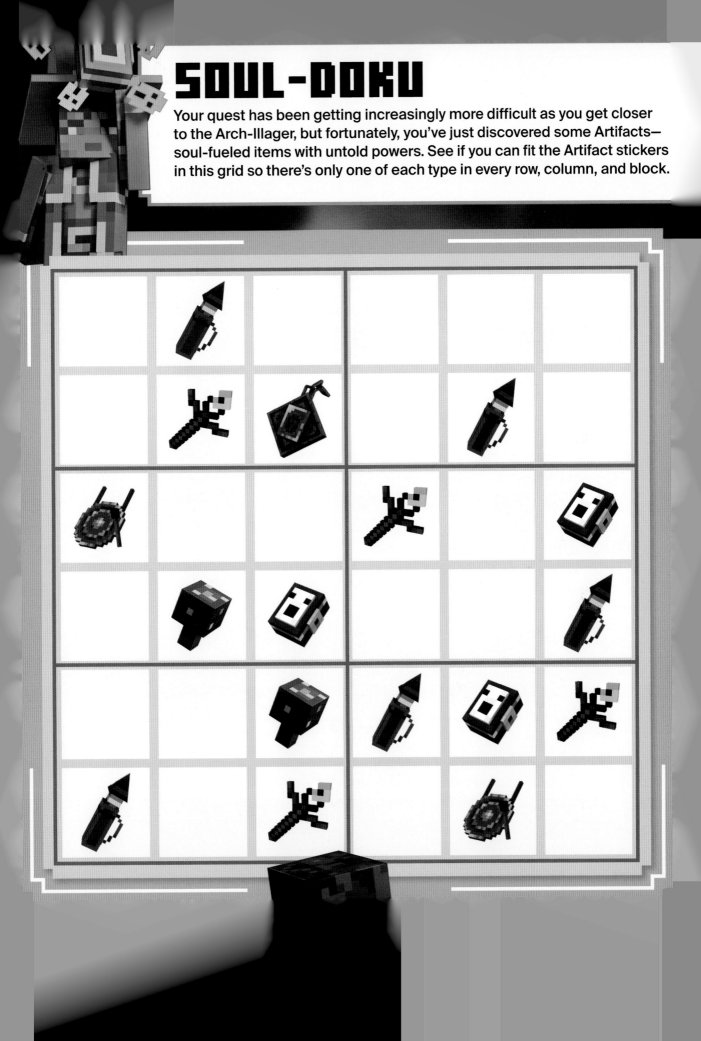

CRAZY COMBO

You've just encountered the devilishly difficult Illagers. After a while, you've started to find a rhythm to battling these vicious mobs. Work out where you should place the correct stickers so that you can use the sequence provided to find a path through the Illagers and keep your combo going.

START

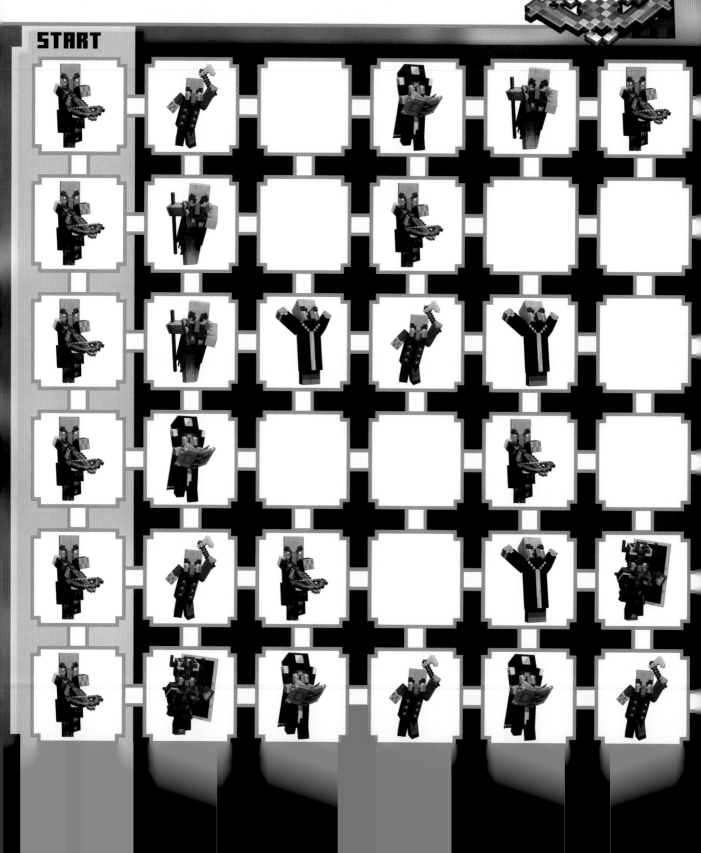

SEQUENCE

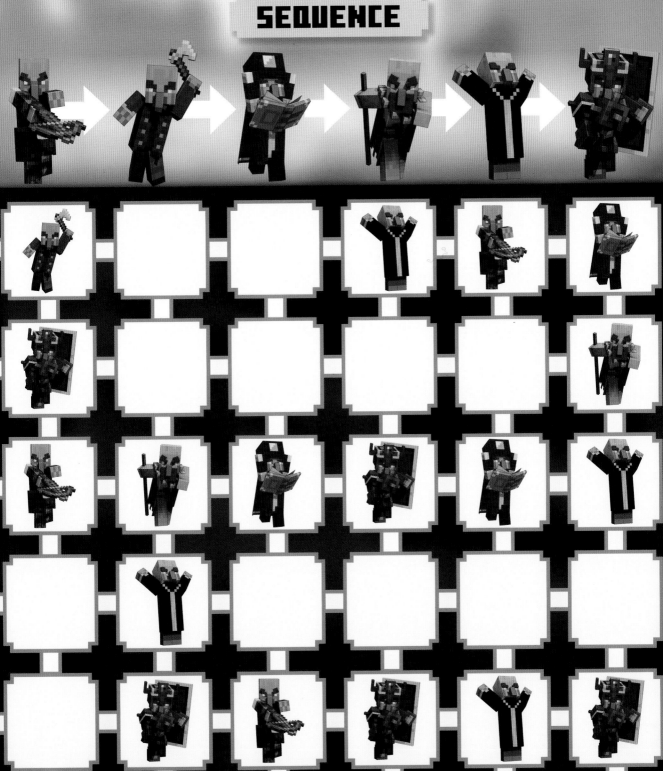

THE INVASION OF PUMPKIN PASTURES

Finally, you've stumbled upon another town, but you're too late. Pumpkin Pastures has been razed by the Arch-Illager's forces. Add some hero stickers to this scene to clear out the Illagers and return peace to the village.

SLIME RANCHER

These pesky slimes won't stop multiplying! You need to split them into more manageable groups. Use the wall stickers on your sheet to separate the slimes into groups. Each group should consist of one large, two medium, and four small slimes.

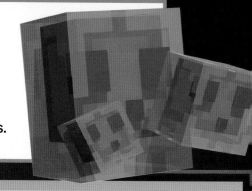

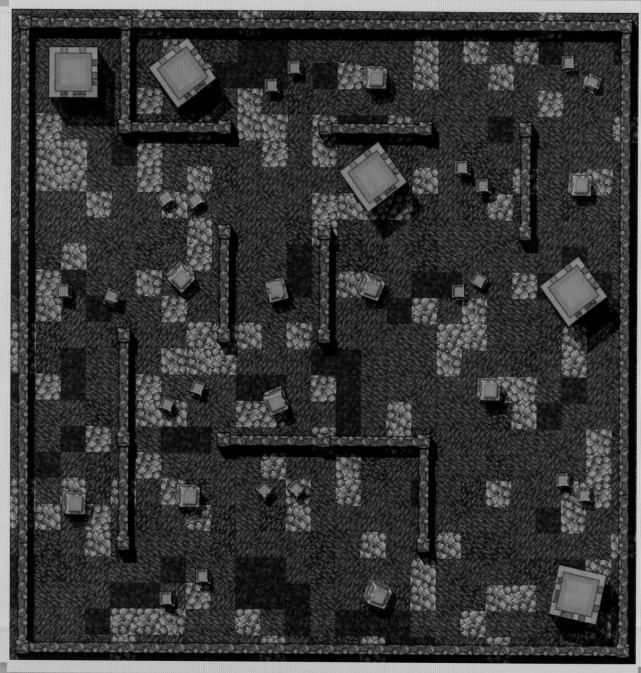

FRIENDLY FACES

Sometimes even a hero needs help! Luckily, there are a number of brave beasts that will aid you on your quest. Read the clues below to help you work out which friendly mob is being described. Then place stickers of each mob so they can join your adventure!

1

In the darkest dungeons and the deepest caves, this little guy scurries around, waiting for an adventurer to pass through and find it. It'll hop on your back if you pick it up but run away again if you take damage.

2

A metallic goliath who likes to smash hostile mobs with its gigantic fists. Some adventurers have claimed they once crafted this mob, but now you'll need a specific Artifact to gain its aid.

3

An elusive mob that carries around a chest full of great treasure. It will try to evade you on its short, porky legs, but heroes who persevere in their pursuit will be richly rewarded.

4

This beast of burden really knows how to help out a hero. If you can summon it with the Wonderful Wheat Artifact, it will use a vicious spitting attack to help fend off Illagers.

5

With the aid of a Tasty Bone, you'll be able to summon this lupine sidekick for a brief period of time. Hostile mobs be warned: its bite is much worse than its howl!

6

A fluttering nocturnal menace, once thought unattainable by heroes of the world. They seem particularly drawn to cave-venturing heroes who wear the Spelunker's Armor.

REDSTONE MINE BREAKOUT

Your journey takes you deep underground to the crimson heart of the Redstone Mines, where you find imprisoned Villagers put to work. Add some hero stickers to fend off the Illagers and free the poor Villagers.

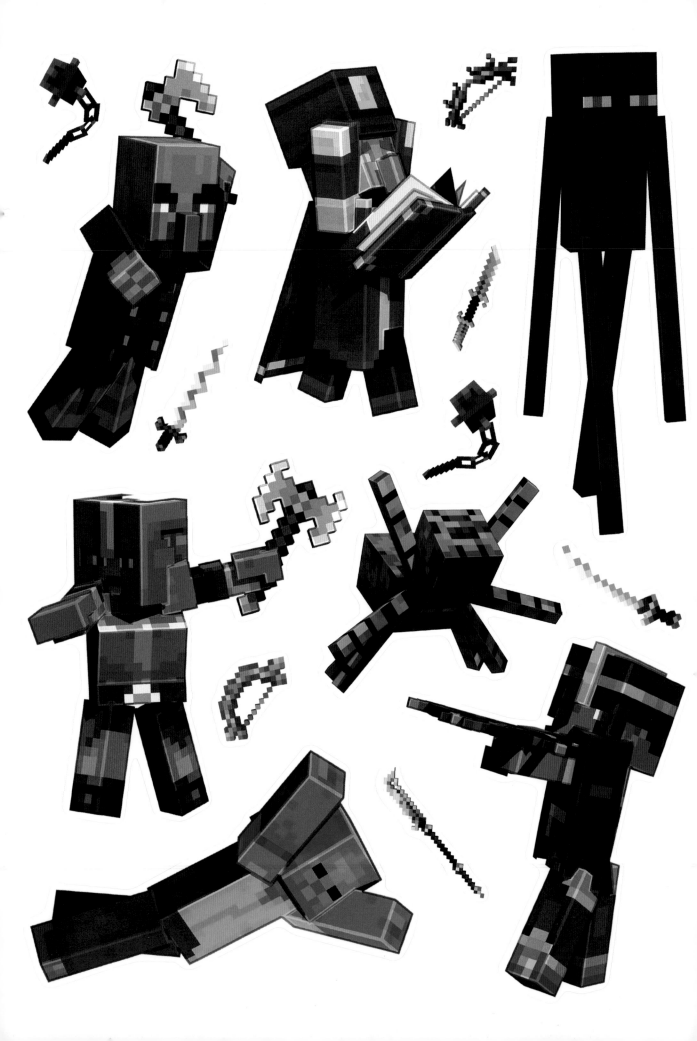

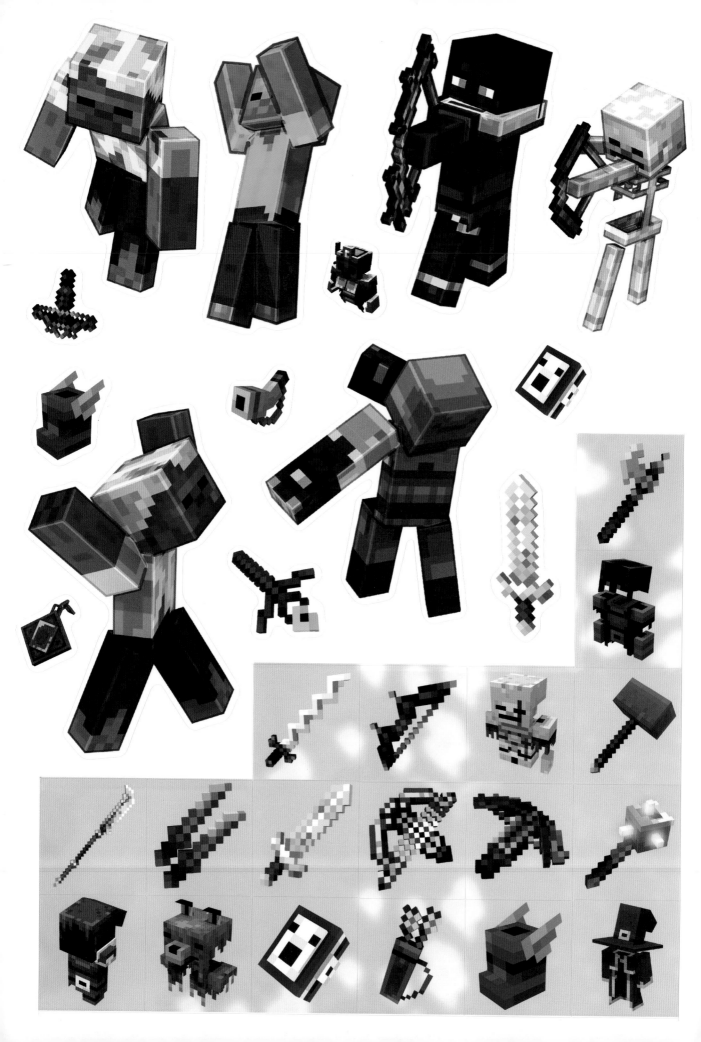

KEY TO THE PUZZLE

On your way out of the mines, you're faced with a locked door. Five key golems scurry around the area, but which one matches the lock exactly? First you need to work out which key golem matches the shape . . . then you need to catch it.

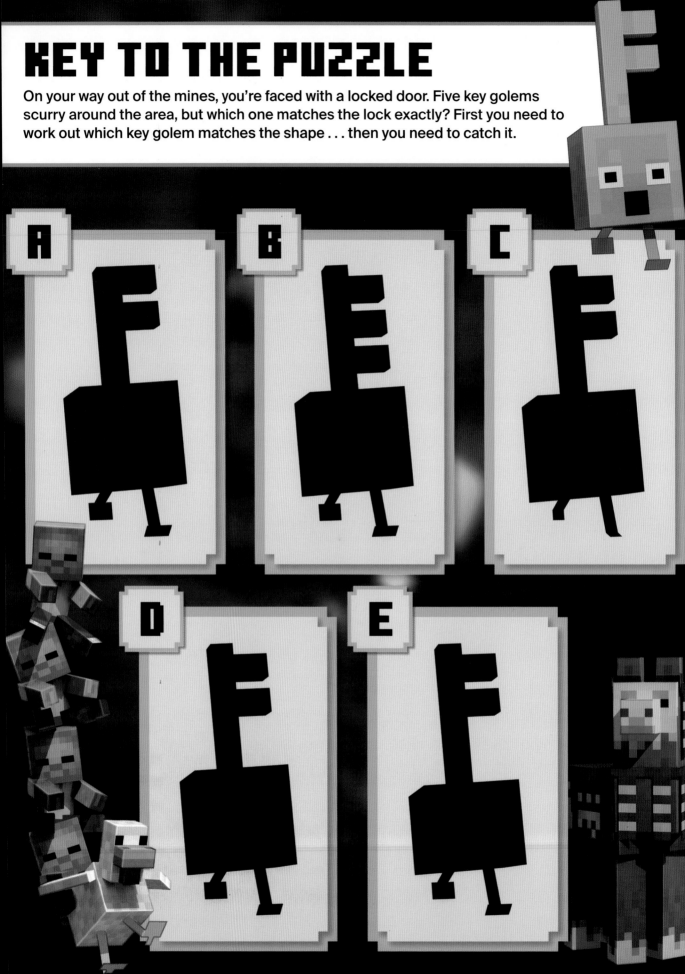

GEOMANCER'S LABYRINTH

The Arch-Illager has released his heavy hitters—he must be getting scared. Most pressingly, a geomancer has complicated your venture by raising a stone maze ahead of you. Can you make it to the other side and put an end to his antics?

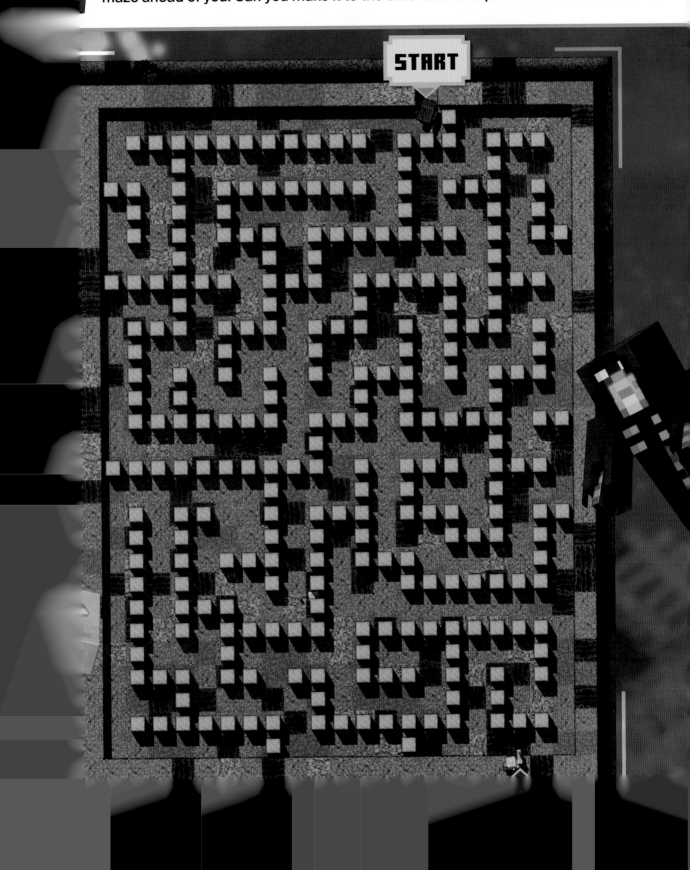

START

NECROMANCER'S LAIR

This once peaceful canyon has been overrun by the necromancer and its undead armada of skeletons, zombies, and husks. Put some hero stickers on the page to send these mobs back to their graves.

AMBUSH AVOIDANCE

After traversing half the world, you're ready to deal with the Arch-Illager . . . but you've heard rumblings of an ambush he has lying in wait for you. Thankfully, you've managed to "extract" a few clues from defeated Illagers as to where this trap might be. Follow the directions from the starting point to discover where the ambush awaits.

START

DIRECTIONS

North - 4	East - 1
East - 2	North - 3
South - 2	West - 1
East - 1	North - 3
North - 2	West - 1
	North - 2

ENCHANTED

Upon reaching Highblock Keep, you're greeted by an enchanter, who is powering up the mobs around it. Follow the flow of the enchanter's magics to identify which mobs are being buffed by the shady Illager.

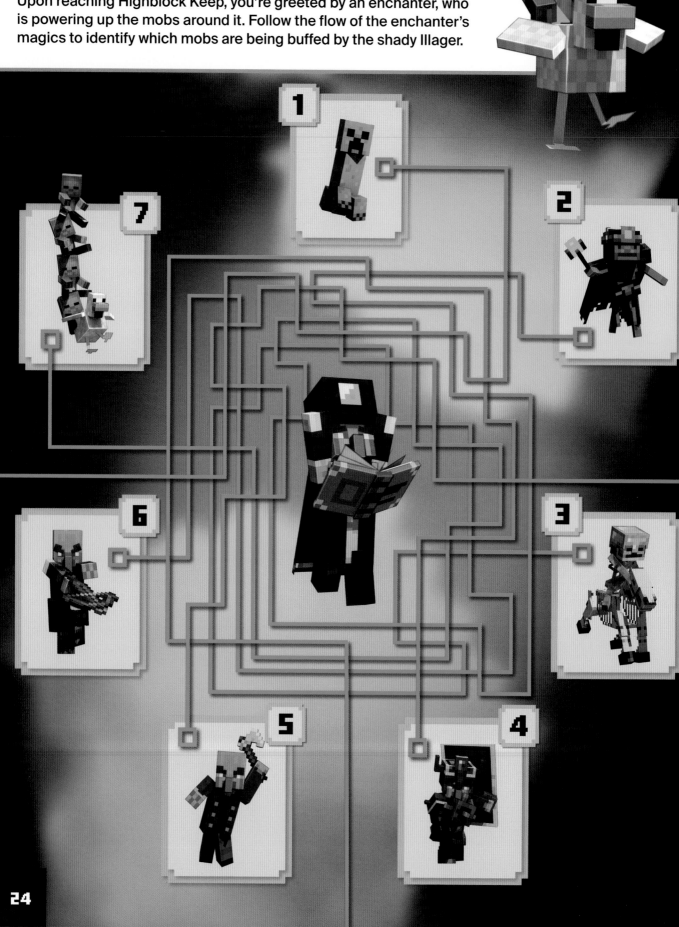

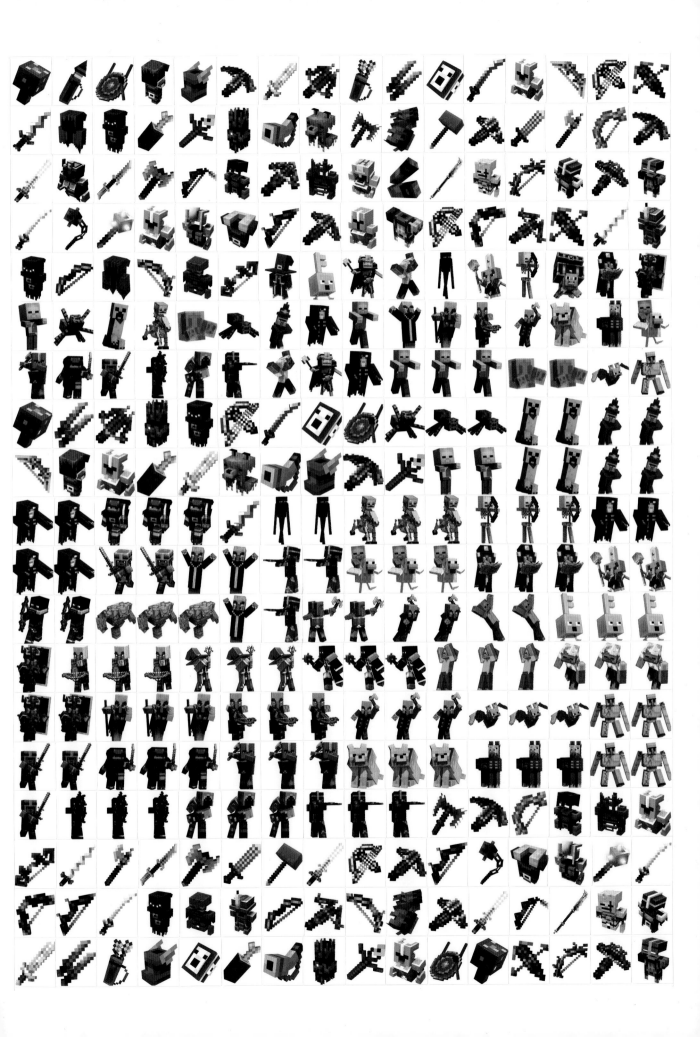

PERPLEXING PLAYSTYLES

You never know what the deadly denizens of Dungeons will throw at you next, so it's always a good idea to try out different ways to play. Use the clues below to work out what's missing. Then add stickers to complete each playstyle.

	SOUL HUNTER	TRICKSTER	ARCHER	HEALER	NINJA
MELEE WEAPON	Eternal Knife				Dark Katana
RANGED WEAPON	Voidcaller	Imploding Crossbow		Sabrewing	
ARMOR	Soul Robe		Mercenary Armor		Spider Armor
ARTIFACT		Wind Horn		Totem of Regeneration	

Clues

- The playstyle that uses the **Boots of Swiftness** does not use the **Eternal Knife**.
- The Ninja does not wield the **Harp Crossbow**.
- The playstyle that wears **Mercenary Armor** also has the melee weapon **Fangs of Frost**.
- The Trickster does not wield the **Diamond Sword** as a melee.

- The **Fox Armor** does not belong to the playstyle that uses the melee weapon **Grave Bane**.
- The **Grave Bane** belongs to the character that wears the **Hunter's Armor**.
- The **Flaming Quiver** Artifact belongs to the Archer.
- The Ninja has a **Butterfly Crossbow** at its disposal.

MISSING ITEMS

Fangs of Frost		Butterfly Crossbow	
Harp Crossbow		Flaming Quiver	
Hunter's Armor		Diamond Sword	
Harvester		Grave Bane	
Boots of Swiftness		Fox Armor	

BATTLE OF THE OBSIDIAN PINNACLE

You're almost at the final battle, but just as you reach the Obsidian Pinnacle, mobs flood out the doors to defend their master's stronghold. Add some heroes to kick some Illager butt and storm the castle!

ROYAL IMPOSTER

In an attempt to preserve itself, the Arch-Illager's last remaining Royal Guard has dressed some innocent Villagers as decoys. Can you tell which one of the Guards below doesn't look like the others? That's the one you need to defeat!

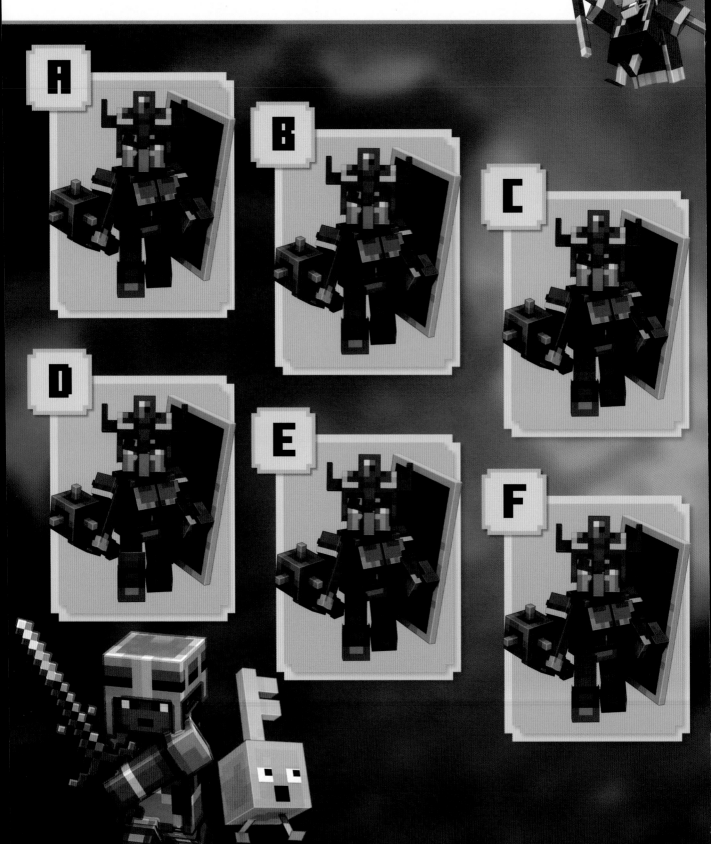

ENDING EVIL'S REIGN

It looks like the Arch-Illager wasn't the villain you had to worry about after all. The hideous Heart of Ender is now the only thing standing in the way of victory. Read each question and place an attack sticker over the correct answer to do an epic combo that will defeat the Heart of Ender.

A	Which type of Illager can control the earth and raise great stone pillars?	NECROMANCER	GEOMANCER	ROMANCER
B	Which helpful golem can help you get through doors?	IRON GOLEM	SNOW GOLEM	KEY GOLEM
C	Which undead mob normally prefers warmer climates?	HUSK	CAVE SPIDER	CHICKEN JOCKEY TOWER
D	The chicken jockey is a combination of a chicken and which other mob?	SPIDER	CREEPER	BABY ZOMBIE
E	What is the name of the Arch-Illager's elite team of protectors?	ROYAL GUARD	MONARCH WARDS	CROWN DEFENDERS
F	What is the name of the castle that the Arch-Illager reigns from?	MIDCUBE BASTION	HIGHBLOCK KEEP	LOWSQUARE FORT

HIDDEN DUNGEONS

Now that the Arch-Illager has been defeated, you can take your time to explore some of the more remote places of the land. You have the names of a few places to visit, but they're all written in the Illager language! Use the code to decipher the name of each place. Then fill in the missing sticker.

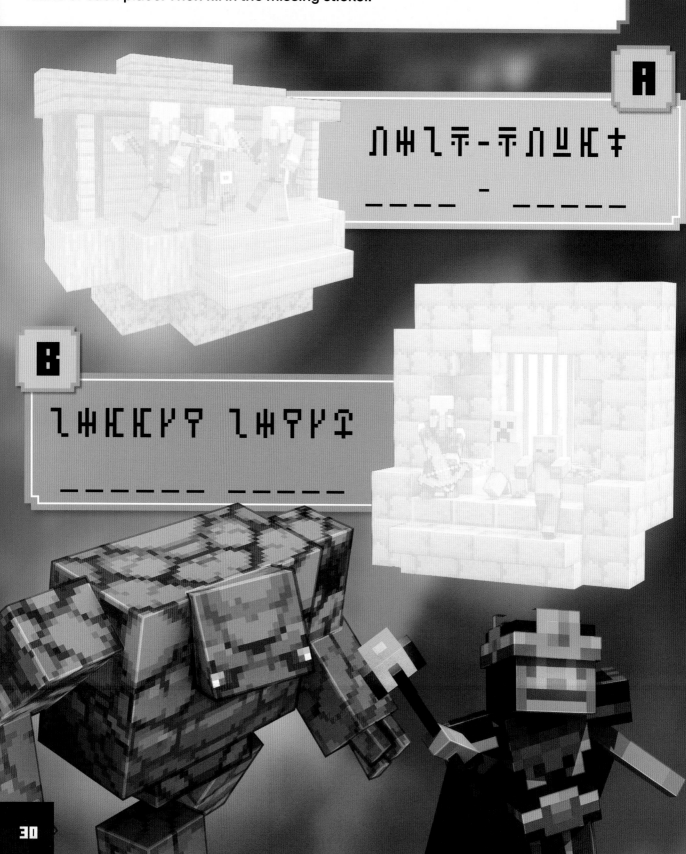

A

∏ Ш Ꮀ Ŧ - Ŧ ∏ Ш Ҝ ╪

_ _ _ _ — - _ _ _ _ _

B

Ꮀ Ш Ҝ Ҝ ⴼ ⵕ   Ꮀ Ш ⵕ ⴼ ⵕ

_ _ _ _ _ _   _ _ _ _ _

30

A	B	C	D	E	F	G	H	I	J	K	L	M	N	O	P	Q	R	S	T	U	V	W	X	Y

C

_____ _____

D

_____ ____

E

_____

ANSWERS

PAGE 2

PAGE 3
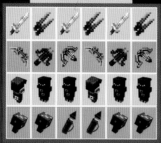

PAGES 6-7
Quits As Cod - **Squid Coast**
Worse Proceed - **Creeper Woods**
PumaPup Stinkers - **Pumpkin Pastures**
Wasps Go Gym - **Soggy Swamp**
I Need Monsters - **Redstone Mines**
Grief Foyer - **Fiery Forge**
Oat Can Cynic - **Cacti Canyon**
Elder Tempest - **Desert Temple**

PAGE 8
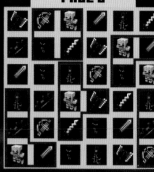

PAGE 9

PAGES 10-11

PAGE 14
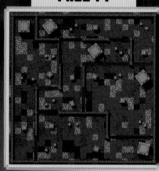

PAGE 15

1, 2, 3, 4, 5, 6

PAGE 18
D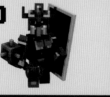

PAGE 19

PAGES 22-23

PAGE 24
2, 3, 6, 7

PAGE 28
D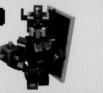

PAGE 25

	SOUL HUNTER	TRICKSTER	ARCHER	HEALER	NINJA
MELEE WEAPON					
RANGED WEAPON					
ARMOR					
ARTIFACT					

PAGE 29
A Geomancer
B Key Golem
C Husk
D Baby Zombie
E Royal Guard
F Highblock Keep

PAGES 30-31
A Arch-Haven
B Creepy Crypt
C Lower Temple
D Soggy Cave
E Underhalls